A Note to Parents and Caregivers:

Read-it! Readers are for children who are just starting on the amazing road to reading. These beautiful books support both the acquisition of reading skills and the love of books.

 The PURPLE LEVEL presents basic topics and objects using high frequency words and simple language patterns.

 The RED LEVEL presents familiar topics using common words and repeating sentence patterns.

 The BLUE LEVEL presents new ideas using a larger vocabulary and varied sentence structure.

 The YELLOW LEVEL presents more challenging ideas, a broad vocabulary, and wide variety in sentence structure.

 The GREEN LEVEL presents more complex ideas, an extended vocabulary range, and expanded language structures.

 The ORANGE LEVEL presents a wide range of ideas and concepts using challenging vocabulary and complex language structures.

When sharing a book with your child, read in short stretches, pausing often to talk about the pictures. Have your child turn the pages and point to the pictures and familiar words. And be sure to reread favorite stories or parts of stories.

There is no right or wrong way to share books with children. Find time to read with your child, and pass on the legacy of literacy.

Adria F. Klein, Ph.D.
Professor Emeritus
California State University
San Bernardino, California

Editor: Christianne Jones
Page Production: Tracy Kaehler
Creative Director: Keith Griffin
Editorial Director: Carol Jones

First American edition published in 2006 by
Picture Window Books
5115 Excelsior Boulevard
Suite 232
Minneapolis, MN 55416
877-845-8392
www.picturewindowbooks.com

First published in 2005 by
Allegra Publishing Limited
Unit 13/15 Quayside Lodge
William Morris Way
Townmead Road
London SW6 2UZ UK

Printed in the United States of America.

Library of Congress Cataloging-in-Publication Data
Law, Felicia.
Rumble meets Vikki Viper / by Felicia Law ; illustrated by Yoon-Mi Pak.
p. cm. — (Read-it! readers)
Summary: While Rumble the dragon and his staff argue with the leader of the
orchestra Rumble hired about whether the violinist, a snake, can come into the
hotel, she slithers in and falls asleep.
ISBN 1-4048-1342-X (hard cover)
[1. Snakes—Fiction. 2. Orchestra—Fiction. 3. Dragons—Fiction. 4. Hotels, motels,
etc.—Fiction.] I. Pak, Yoon Mi, ill. II. Title. III. Series.

PZ7.L41835Rumv 2005
[E]—dc22   2005027177

Rumble Meets Vikki Viper

by Felicia Law
illustrated by Yoon-Mi Pak

Special thanks to our advisers for their expertise:

Adria F. Klein, Ph.D.
Professor Emeritus, California State University
San Bernardino, California

Susan Kesselring, M.A.
Literacy Educator
Rosemount–Apple Valley–Eagan (Minnesota) School District

PICTURE WINDOW BOOKS
Minneapolis, Minnesota

This is the life of a cool, young dragon named Rumble. When his grandma leaves her run-down cave to him, Rumble sets about making it into a four-star hotel. He doesn't do it all alone. He has help from a picky hotel inspector and an annoying spider named Shelby.

Vikki Viper just wants to play
her violin in Rumble's Cave Hotel
orchestra, but Rumble doesn't
like snakes. Eli Elephant, the
orchestra's conductor, does
everything he can to convince
Rumble to let Vikki into his hotel.
Will Rumble change his mind?

Rumble was in a bad mood. He stood at the entrance of his hotel blowing large, angry red flames and stomping his foot on the ground.

"No!" he said as he stomped.
"No! No! No!"

8

"But Vikki Viper plays the violin," said Eli Elephant, "and the orchestra needs a violin player."

"I don't care," roared Rumble angrily. "I don't like snakes."

"Neither do I," said Shelby Spider. "In fact, nobody likes snakes."

"Snake soup!" grunted Wally Warthog.
"That's not bad."

"Snakeskin handbags," purred Penny
Panther. "They're nice."

"No!" said Rumble. "No! No! No!"

"Vipers eat toads,"
said Todd Toad.

"And birds," said Milly
the Maid and Chester
the Chef.

"And rabbits,"
said Randy Rabbit.

"But Vikki Viper is a good snake," said Eli Elephant. "And she plays the violin."

"No," Rumble told Eli Elephant. "Look, everyone agrees with me. No viper! No violin!"

13

"That's final," said Rumble. "There will be no snakes in my hotel."

But he was wrong. Vikki Viper was already in the hotel. She had slithered in when all the fuss and shouting had started. If nobody wanted to help her stay at the hotel, she would help herself. She would find something to eat and somewhere to sleep. She would show them she didn't need an invitation.

15

Nobody had seen her enter the hotel because, like all vipers, she moved quickly and quietly.

Nobody had seen her slither over the stones.

Nobody had seen her creep across the carpet.

Nobody had seen her snuggle up on the sofa.

Next, she sneaked into the kitchen to find something to eat.

Chester the Chef had left some porridge on the table.

"Perfect!" Vikki said as she ate up all of the porridge.

19

Feeling very full from the porridge, Vikki
Viper decided to climb the stairs and look
for somewhere to sleep.

Vikki found an empty bedroom at the end
of the hall.

"Perfect!" she said as she curled herself into
a neat coil and fell fast asleep.

And because vipers hide themselves against their backgrounds, she turned a lovely summery color. Her skin looked like a summer garden—just like the bedspread.

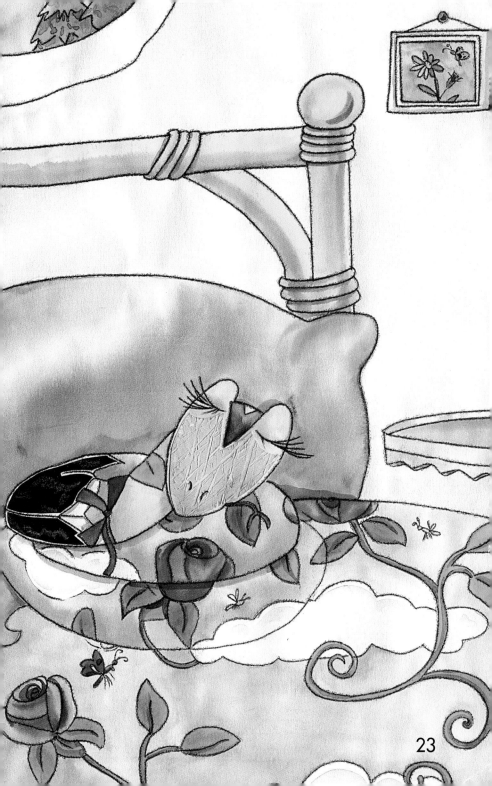

23

She didn't wake up until she heard the orchestra playing. It was playing an old-fashioned tune that sounded very odd because the melody was missing.

"No! No! No!" she heard Rumble shout. "It sounds dreadful! There's no melody."

"No viper means no violin. No violin means no melody," said Eli Elephant.

"Oh, all right then," said Rumble. "Maybe we've been a bit unkind. Let's find Vikki Viper and apologize."

The orchestra hunted high and low, looking
in all the places a viper likes to go—under
rocks, in tall grasses, curled around branches
high up in trees.

They hunted in the kitchen, up and down the stairs, and in all of the bedrooms. At last they found Vikki, snuggled up on the bed.

"We're sorry for being unkind," sniffed Rumble. "We really do need a violin in the orchestra. There's no melody without you."

Vikki Viper accepted Rumble's apology. She took her place in the orchestra. As everyone listened to the music, Vikki changed her skin from a hot red jazz color to a cool blues color and then to a mellow yellow color.

What a performance!

More *Read-it!* Readers

Bright pictures and fun stories help you practice your reading skills. Look for more books at your level.

Alex and Sarah 1-4048-1352-7

Alex and the Team Jersey 1-4048-1024-2

Alex and Toolie 1-4048-1027-7

Clever Cat 1-4048-0560-5

Felicio's Incredible Invention 1-4048-1030-7

Flora McQuack 1-4048-0561-3

Izzie's Idea 1-4048-0644-X

Joe's Day at Rumble's Cave Hotel 1-4048-1339-X

Naughty Nancy 1-4048-0558-3

Parents Do the Weirdest Things! 1-4048-1031-5

The Princess and the Frog 1-4048-0562-1

The Princess and the Tower 1-4048-1184-2

Rumble Meets Harry Hippo 1-4048-1338-1

Rumble Meets Lucas Lizard 1-4048-1334-9

Rumble Meets Randy Rabbit 1-4048-1337-3

Rumble Meets Shelby Spider 1-4048-1286-5

Rumble Meets Todd Toad 1-4048-1340-3

Rumble the Dragon's Cave 1-4048-1353-5

Rumble's Famous Granny 1-4048-1336-5

The Truth About Hansel and Gretel 1-4048-0559-1

Willie the Whale 1-4048-0557-5

Looking for a specific title or level? A complete list of *Read-it!* Readers is available on our Web site:
www.picturewindowbooks.com